Tempted

One Handed Reads
Book 4

Dee Lish

Prologue

This could not be happening. He'd better be dying to have stood me up like this. I stormed to Noah's house and banged repeatedly on his front door. When Mrs Redmond finally answered, I barrelled past her, racing upstairs to find him.

"Noah!" I called, lunging through his bedroom door.

"Gemma!" his mum called after me. "He's not here!" she told me as she entered his room, finally catching up with me.

"Where is he?"

She moved towards me and put her hand on my arm. "He's gone, love."

"Gone where?" I didn't understand. "When will he be back?"

Mrs Redmond looked at me sadly; I could see the pity on her face. "He's gone away for a while, love. He won't be back for quite some time."

The room started to swim. "What do you mean? Where... where is he?"

"He's not coming back, Gemma."

No. This could not be happening. I loved him. He was

my soulmate. *He couldn't just leave me; he wouldn't. I pushed back past his mum, ran down the stairs, and back out the front door.*

I pulled my phone from my pocket and scrolled to Noah's number, hitting call. A tone sounded in my ear and a voice announced, 'The number you have dialled has not been recognised'. My eyes burned. I cancelled the call and typed out his number manually, just in case.

'The number you have dialled has not been recognised.'

"No!" *I screamed and took off running. I didn't know where I was going. Away from there; away from the truth, perhaps. I needed to escape from the overwhelming tidal wave of heartbreak that was threatening to swallow me whole. Noah was gone. I didn't know where, I didn't know how long he would be gone, and I had no way of contacting him anymore. It was over. The thought made me stumble, and I came crashing to the pavement on my knees. My embarrassment was only amplified by a guy I knew from school witnessing the whole horrific event. He rushed over to help me up.*

"Jesus. Are you okay?" *he asked as he put his arm around me and pulled me off the ground.*

"I'm okay." *I felt my face burn. I accepted his help as he manoeuvred me to a bench.*

"That knee looks bad." *He pulled a tissue from his pocket.* "It's clean," *he added, dabbing the nasty graze on my leg.* "Gemma, right?"

I nodded, my eyes stinging from the myriad of emotions surging through me. Heartbreak. Embarrassment. The pain in my knee.

"I'm..." *he started.*

"Daniel. I know."

A small smile graced his lips. "Dan. My mum is a nurse.

She has a great first aid kit in the house. It's just over there. Can you make it that far?" He pointed to the house just a few doors down. I nodded.

"Maybe you'll tell me what happened over a cup of tea?" He smiled, putting his arm around me and helping me hobble over to his house for some tea and sympathy.

"Gemma, are you even listening to me?" Fiona says, poking me in the side as I stare at my phone.

"What?" I ask distractedly.

"I said are you listening to me, but I think you just answered that one." I glance up at her. "What the fuck is so interesting on Facebook?" She looks over the edge of my phone screen to see what's keeping my interest from the latest gossip on her love life.

I press the button on my phone before setting it back on the table in front of us. "Nothing. It's just a friend request from someone I've not heard from in years," I reply, trying to sound like it's the most natural thing in the world.

She gives me that look, and I know I'm already screwed. My mistake has been made and I've shared too much. She won't let this go now.

"Who?" She grins. "It's not an old flame, is it?"

"Oh, shut up, Fi!" Don't get me wrong, I love Fiona; she's the best assistant a girl could have. However, sometimes, as much as we're friends, she doesn't know when to stop and just leave it be.

"Ohh, it is an old flame!" She smirks, knowing full well that I realise my mistake as much as she does. Yep, definitely not going to let this drop now. I'm fucked. I give a moment's thought to which is going to be the lesser of two evils; telling her now, or letting her drag it out of me like it's some sort of game. Maybe the former is better.

Just tell her and get it over, Gem.

"Fine. Yes, it's an old flame. The oldest one there can be, as it happens." I sigh in defeat.

"Not the squaddie? The soul mate, love of your life, before he fucked off and you met Daniel?"

Trust Fi to be as blunt as a brick to the side of the head. "Yes, that one. Only Noah wasn't a squaddie, not really, last time I saw him."

"When he came back, and you were already with Daniel. You were like twenty-one?" she asks, eager to get the story straight in her mind.

"Yes!" I reply, my patience growing thin.

"Sorry. Continue."

I nod a curt thank you for being allowed to finish what I was saying. "Yes, it's Noah. No, I haven't seen him since I was twenty-one and about to get married. And now he's sent me a friend request on Facebook."

"I see," she says. "Gemma, if he's just an old flame, why are you so worked up about it already?"

I think about it, and I think about Noah. I realise my mistake hasn't been just telling Fiona what I was so distracted over. It's the flurry of thoughts and feelings running around in my mind over the mere sight of his name and profile picture in my friend request list on Facebook.

"What the hell did you think would happen, Noah? It's been three fucking years!" I screamed at him.

He sat there, his head in his hands, looking like his world had just fallen apart. Maybe it had, but I instantly pushed that thought out of my head. Nope, not my problem. I wasn't the one to leave.

"Fuck! I don't know, Gem. Part of me didn't think that far ahead. I guess I always had this mental image of a great reunion where I come back to find you still here, single, waiting..." His voice trailed off, and I stared at him.

"Are you for real? You thought you would leave me without a word or reason, and I would somehow just be sitting here pining away for you? Waiting for your glorious return with open arms?"

He stood, ready to fight his side. "I know I didn't say anything. I know I just left. I didn't think I was fucking good enough, okay? I didn't think I was the man you needed, and I left to become something more. To make myself the kind of man that you deserved."

"What I deserved, Noah, was a boyfriend who didn't just up and leave and break my fucking heart. What I deserved was, at the very least, an explanation of where the hell you were going!"

He started to move towards me and took my hand. I pulled back angrily. I didn't want him touching me. He left me, and I was supposed to be happy he was back? I couldn't believe how ridiculous he was being.

"Gem," he pleaded.

I can't do this; it's not fair. I was getting married in three weeks. Daniel was my rock when I felt so lost. He looked after me when Noah left, and he grew into more. He deserved better than this. I couldn't just drop him so close to the wedding and go back to the idiot who left me.

"Noah, you tore my heart out. You were my whole world, and you disappeared without a trace. Daniel was there for me. Daniel put me back together. Daniel would never leave me like you did."

"So he's safe?" Noah bit.

I stormed towards him, my finger up in his face. I wanted to scream at him. I wanted to slap him. Instead, I shouted at him. "Don't you ever put him down. He might not be what you were to me, but he's still better than you. He would never treat me like you did," I said, my finger punctuating my words.

Noah grabbed my wrist and pulled me against him. I was overloaded. I wanted to push him away, and before I got the chance to process it, his mouth was on mine. I responded, the last three years temporarily drifting away. I moulded against him, tasted his tongue in my mouth, and all I could think of was Daniel, and the betrayal I was committing.

I pushed Noah off me with everything I had. My hand came across his face and then covered my mouth in shock at my reaction to both him and what I just did. "Get the fuck out of here, Noah."

His lips parted. He thought about what to say and then decided against it. His hands were stuffed into the pockets of his jeans, his head hanging, and he walked away. As he did, he bumped into Daniel. "Sorry," he muttered.

"My bad," Daniel replied.

Noah was gone. Again. Daniel walked over, wrapped his arms around me, and kissed my forehead. Right then and there, I was split down the middle. Part of me belonged to Noah, and part of me belonged to Daniel. I wasn't sure that would ever change.

Chapter One

There are times when I love my job. I love meeting new people. The networking, the interaction, everything. But there are also times when I've been as busy as I have with this wedding expo when I just can't wait to get back to the hotel, put on some jeans and a t-shirt, and go and enjoy the bar food and a quiet drink.

Fiona is down with the flu. She was meant to be with me, but after she called me on Wednesday night, I told her to get her arse into bed and not move from there. The plan we had for the event was all but sorted, and it wouldn't be too much extra for me to do it solo. Tough, but not impossible. I had networked, I had chatted, I had sorted out some new contacts, and generated interest in the wedding planning business I run, and things were generally going well. I have earned the break tonight. Tomorrow, I'll head home, and I can't wait to see Daniel. He's been at a conference in the United States for two weeks, so by the time I get home tomorrow, it will have been seventeen days since I last saw him. Even after nineteen years together, I still look forward to getting home to my lovely husband. I grab my phone, my room key card, and my business credit card, and leave my room for the bar.

I settle myself into the little nook in the corner I found the first night and quietly enjoy a glass of red wine while I watch the latest match in the Rugby Union Six Nations. England is uncharacteristically kicking the ass of Wales; something I'll have great fun teasing Fiona about later when I phone her to tell her how it went today. I lose myself in the sights of big, strapping men running about a pitch, being rough as fuck with each other while attempting to score. It reminds me of Daniel and cold Saturdays spent watching him play rugby for his university team and the hot baths and sports massages that followed. Damn, I miss my husband.

By the time the match is over, my glass is empty, and I head to the bar to order some food and another glass of wine. The bar is a little busier than usual, but I just assume that's because it's a Friday night in a vibrant town. I wait to get the attention of the girl behind the bar.

I'm aware of a man standing beside me, and I'm about to order when the girl at the bar walks straight past me to the man, serving him first. I've never been one to shy away from telling someone they're wrong, and this certainly isn't the time for me to start. I'm hangry, and I turn to face the miserable, queue-jumping bastard.

"Uh, excuse me?" I start, but when the face who dared to take my place in the bar queue hierarchy turns to face me, I'm utterly floored. A sentiment mirrored in the expression of said bastard. In an instant, my disgust at his behaviour melts, and it's replaced with an awareness of the tingling running through every inch of my body.

Of course, I'm face-to-face with none other than Noah fucking Redmond. All I can think about to distract me from the betrayal of my body's reaction to him is how Fiona is going to have a shit fit when she hears the latest feedback I have from the expo.

Chapter Two

"Gemma?" My name just rolls off his tongue, and I can feel the skin prickle at the back of my neck. His voice is older; a richer baritone than when I last saw him. He's taller than I remember. His eyes haven't lost a bit of that cheeky sparkle they had and are still a gorgeous chocolate brown I could get lost looking at. I do, in fact, for a second, and I'm sure I must be blushing a little when I snap out of it and look at him.

"Fucking hell. Noah Redmond." I attempt to smile at him but then overthink it. I'm sure I must look like a right twat. Before I have the time to overthink that too and ask myself why I care if a man I haven't heard from in decades thinks I'm a twat, his arms are around me, and he pulls me close against him.

"Christ, I haven't seen you in years," he murmurs against my neck.

Alarm bells are going off in my body, and in my mind, already dragging me in two different directions. I feel it. I melt into his hug, and his body gratefully accepts it. Every inch of me is humming with energy, and so much of me wants to let whatever it is go wherever the fuck it's going. On the other side of that equation, my brain has a judgemental bitch looking at me, asking me what the fuck I think I'm doing getting so turned on by a man who is practically a stranger, and sure as shit isn't my husband.

Judgy Bitch wins this round. I pull myself back from Noah's hug, and for a split second, I swear I see disappointment flash across his features. His eyes burn into me and I feel them everywhere.

"So," I say, attempting to diffuse the situation. I need to encourage some kind of normal, friendly, innocent chitchat between us instead of this sexually charged nuke threatening to implode and wipe out everyone in its wake.

"Can I get you a drink?"

"What have you been up to?"

We blurt the words in unison. The tension is broken and we settle a little.

"Thanks. I'd love a glass of Rioja." I smile at him. He motions to the same bar wench who had ignored me in favour of him just minutes before and orders both of us a drink.

"Did you eat?" he asks. I tell him no and explain I was about to order when he so rudely interrupted. He smiles at me, and I feel the tension sneaking back in, only this time it's a little different. It's strangely exciting, a bare naked thrill. *Oh, yeah. Bare naked, Gem. Great thought; now look where your mind will go.* Judgy Bitch starts again. I tell Noah the food I want, and he puts in the order before paying and moving back to me.

"Where were you sitting?" he asks, and I motion for him to follow me back to my little isolated nook. The skin on my neck is prickling again. I can feel his eyes on me; I can see that no one else is around where I've been sitting. I think about how I'm about to be tucked into a corner with a man who makes my body hum with just his presence. I am so screwed.

Chapter Three

"So, how long have you been married to... Nathaniel, wasn't it?" Noah asks.

"Daniel," I correct. Some things never change. That old 'I didn't really listen to his name, even though I know what he's called' routine.

"Oh, yeah. Daniel. Sorry," he sheepishly replies.

I smirk, feeling the victory in him seeming jealous about who I've been happily married to for years now. "Seventeen years," I inform him. "About three weeks after I last saw you. May twentieth. We just had our anniversary last month."

He nods, and I can feel the something unsaid. There's something more he wants to ask, but whatever it is, he stops himself from asking it.

"What about you?" I ask him, not thinking about the answer I might hear until he says it.

"Still single," he tells me, and a sense of relief I didn't know I wanted washes over me.

"How come?"

"Honestly?" he asks, and I shrug. "Because I once had

the perfect woman, and I lost her, and since then, no one else has ever measured up."

"Oh, right," I say, trying to sound nonchalant. I want to ask who she was. If he met her in the army or after. By the look on his face, it appears as though he's about to query that I don't understand who he means, and I realise.

She's me.

"Ohhh..." Panic takes over. "Look, Noah, I've been happily marr–" I start, and he takes my hand.

"No, don't," he reassures me. "I don't mean it like that. I know you're married. I don't mean to make you feel bad, I just... I've never been able to hide anything from you, Gem." His thumb rubs over the back of my hand, and I look at it and then at him. There's a loaded moment when I feel that pull towards him start in my chest. In an attempt to do anything but give in to it, I pull my hand from his like he's scorched me.

Both of us sit in silence. I grab my glass of wine and knock it back in one long gulp. He takes the glass from me and gets up. "Let me get you another," he mumbles almost bashfully, and walks away to the bar.

Judgy Bitch launches into her next 'pep talk.' My mind runs wild between how much I want him to keep touching me, and how much I need to stop whatever the fuck it is I think I'm doing. Say goodnight, lovely to see him, and escape to the comfort of my room. ALONE. I'll head home to my husband, where I can fuck his brains out and remind myself—as if I needed reminding—why I love him, and why we are still happily married after so many years. I win this round because when he returns to the nook with my next glass of red, I stay where I am, sitting beside him, chatting as casually as I can with him.

* * *

Time passes, drinks flow, and we settle into a comfortable patter with each other. We talk about what we do, and almost everything that has happened in the seventeen years that have passed since we saw each other last. The more I drink, the flirtier I get; the occasional slap on his shoulder when I laugh at something he says. I can see it happening, and as much as I can hear the rant Judgy Bitch is having in my head, the alcohol has dulled her down to a wordless roar in the corner. I can no longer make out her words, and if I'm honest, I no longer want to.

I catch him in a look. "What?" I ask with a smirk.

"I've missed you, Gem."

I stare at him. I want to smile at his confession. I want to admit that I've missed him too, but I can't.

"Sorry. I didn't mean to make you uncomfortable again. I don't mean to spoil this," he says gesturing between us.

I grab his hand this time. "No! No... you haven't," I reassure him, and instead of letting go of him, I let our hands drop into the space between us, our fingers naturally entwining. He looks down at them and back up to me. His thumb moves back over mine. I squeeze his fingers and the pull starts. I suddenly realise his face is moving towards mine, and instead of moving away, I help him to close the gap between us. Seconds stretch out as my body tingles, waiting for that moment until his lips touch mine.

My phone rings. I look down at it and see Dan's name flashing on the screen. *Well, shit.*

Chapter Four

"Sorry about that," I say as I plonk my arse back down onto the seat beside him.

"No, it's fine," he says, with a smile that doesn't quite reach his eyes.

"Today was a big deal for me, and he was just calling to see how things had gone."

"Gem, he's your husband. He's allowed to call you and see how you got on without you needing to explain to me." There is an edge to his tone, and all I feel is regret. He had been about to kiss me, and what's more, I had been about to kiss him back. I wanted to. Hell, I still want to. But fate reminded me I'm a married woman just when I needed it most.

"I know. But... I just... Oh... I think I've had too much to drink. Maybe I should just go up to my room and head to bed." I sigh.

I watch as he fights with himself over what to say next. "I'll walk up with you. To my room, I mean."

Another flash of disappointment sinks over me. I shouldn't want him. I shouldn't feel as turned on as I do.

But there's something about Noah Redmond that does what it has always done. It speaks to my soul. It whispers to my pussy.

"Okay," I murmur and stand up. The alcohol mixes with my neediness, and I stumble. Noah's hand is instantly at the small of my back to steady me against him.

"Uh, thanks," I say, pulling myself back from him. I'm trying to take the hint fate has given me and have some common sense, even if I no longer have decency. His hand slips from its hold of me, and he motions for me to lead the way. Slowly and carefully, I walk over to the elevators.

The last of the crowd from the elevator leaves, and there's just Noah and me getting in.

"What floor?" he asks me, his fingers hovering over the buttons for the floors.

"Six," I tell him.

He raises an eyebrow. "Me too. Funny coincidence."

I can't breathe anymore. I'm holding it because, if I let it out, I'll give myself away. So, I stand here, thinking about him being on the same floor as me, and the fact that he might be in the room just next door, and I wait.

The lift arrives on the sixth floor, and I head out of it, letting out my breath. Noah follows me. "Are you down here, too?" I ask.

"Just a bit further."

I stop outside 606. "This is me," I say and fish the key card out of my back pocket. I put it into the little slot about twenty different ways, and it just refuses to open the bloody door. Again, his hands are on mine.

"Give it here." He smirks.

I can't say anything. I'm too busy thinking about him touching me again, and how there's a nice big bed on the other side of this door.

Noah puts the key card in the lock, pulls it out, and the green light flashes instantly. He pushes the door open, puts the card into the slot on the wall, and flicks on the light. "You go and get some sleep," he tells me.

"Thank you." I smile at him. We pause, staring at each other, static swimming in the air around us.

"It really was lovely to see you again, Gem." He smiles at me. "Sweet dreams." He pulls the door closed behind him, leaving me standing here. Hesitancy and yearning battle in my body. I want to go after him. I want to at least find out his room number, but I find myself rooted to the spot. Minutes pass, and I realise it's too late. I flop on the bed, kick off my heels, and grab the TV remote from the bedside table. At least I can view my blues away with some *Real Housewives of Orange County*. I sigh. Judgy Bitch can be heard again. She thinks my frustrations are just what I need to teach me a damn lesson. Less whoring, more wifeing.

I'm just about comfortable when the door to my room is knocked. I sigh, get off the bed, and stomp to the door. I pull it open with a swift tug, and a split-second later, my body is engulfed by another's. Lips are on mine, and the second they touch me, that familiar feeling creeps all over me. Noah. Noah's lips are on mine. Noah's hands have just cupped my arse. Noah's tongue is slipping between my lips and teasing my own tongue.

Our kiss intensifies. I pull him hard against me and grab at the back of his t-shirt; I need to find his skin beneath it. When I do, I'm rewarded with a moan against my lips, his hips rocking against me, his hands sliding up my back and pulling me hard against him.

My head swims, and he pries his mouth from mine. "I'm sorry, Gem. I just... I had to fucking kiss you."

I can't fight it anymore. "Fuck, I've missed you," I tell him, and his lips collide with mine again. Now, I don't care. Fuck the consequences. In this moment, I have never wanted anything more. In this moment, Noah Redmond has me utterly tempted. Up until this very moment, I would always have said that I'm a happily married woman. I still am, but it's Noah, and the same pull that has always been there draws me in, and I just need to be with him.

Chapter Five

His t-shirt is the first thing to hit the floor in my hotel bedroom. I need to let my eyes feast on everything that's below it. I need to be reminded of just how good he looks. I need to run my hands over every inch of his broad chest and shoulders, to enjoy my fingertips on his chest hair, just like I did all those years ago. There's more of it now than there was when we were teenagers. He's more muscular too. A most welcome side effect from his years of service in the army, I'm sure.

Every inch of me is crying out for every inch of him. It's like some strange floodgate has been opened after years of being pent-up and denied. I need Noah right now more than I need air.

I'm craving skin-on-skin contact with him when he lifts my t-shirt over my head. Once I'm free of it, he discards it on the floor with his. His eyes scorch me as they take in every bare inch of skin on my upper body before finally lingering on my breasts.

His hands cup my breasts through my bra, and his mouth descends between my tits, sucking on the exposed flesh of each one in turn. I think I've given Judgy Bitch a stroke; she's silent now, and I'm enjoying the utterly blissful sensations flowing through me with the touch of Noah's hands and mouth.

His hands slide around my body to my back, and with a skilful flick, my bra comes undone. I raise an eyebrow playfully, and Noah grins. "A lad can pick up a few skills in twenty years, you know."

Now it's my turn to grin. "Oh, really?" I ask, wondering what other new skills he might have.

Noah laughs. "Wait and see." He winks, and I flush with heat, my pussy tightening.

His mouth skims my neck as his hands lazily trail over my back. Goosebumps prickle over my skin as Noah's mouth traces over me, down towards my breasts.

A long moan falls from my lips as he lifts my breast with his hand and encloses my nipple in his mouth. I lift my hand to the back of his head, holding his mouth exactly where it is. He pulls me tighter into his mouth in response. He breaks contact only briefly to swap to my other breast.

"Oh, fuck, Noah!" I moan. His eyes make contact with mine, and I witness the pure, unadulterated lust reflected in them. In that instant, the entire world disappears. Nothing else exists but Noah and me.

"You are even better than I remember," he tells me, and instead of dismissing it like I would if Daniel said it, I absorb the words and let them wash over me as truth. I guess seventeen years of marriage will do that. It's not that I don't believe my husband, I've just heard it so often that it no longer registers as a genuine compliment. Noah lowers his face to mine, his lips brushing against my mouth lightly, teasing me, making me need more.

I cup his face in my hands, a day's worth of scruff

prickling my palms. "Seventeen years wear well on you," I tell him, and I'm rewarded once again with his mouth on mine and his hand running over my bare back.

As our kiss deepens, his hands roam down to my ass where he grabs a handful. My hips gain a mind of their own and roll against his grasp. Noah responds by pulling me harder against him. I can feel how hard he is through our jeans, and I'm all the more aware that I'm wearing far too many clothes even now.

I instinctively wrap a leg around his hip, needing more contact with him against all the right places, and he reassigns a hand from my ass to hold my leg. His hand firmly rubs along my thigh, and the need for more and the constant passionate kissing makes my head spin. I'm overwhelmed. I'm out of control. I am so turned on right now that I could spontaneously combust.

I push Noah back, and he lets my leg drop back down so I can get my foot on the floor.

"What's wrong?" he asks.

I hold up a hand to stop him from saying more. He doesn't need to. "Just give me a second. It's all good, I'm just a little too..." my voice trails off, unable to explain what I really mean.

"It's okay, Gem. You don't have to do this. I know you're not free. I wouldn't want you to do anything you would regret."

I know he means it. God bless Noah Redmond because I know that, right now, if I told him I couldn't do it, if I told him to put his t-shirt back on and leave, he would. Judgy Bitch rings out clearly in my head. *Tell him then...* But I can't. I look at him and shake my head. I know if I don't do what I'm about to do, that would be my regret. Walking away from this beautiful man would be positively impossible. I just need a few seconds to take stock, collect my thoughts, and calm my nerves.

My nerves are still shot, but I can't *not* do this. I need to do this. I need to feel this, I need to feel him, even if it's just for tonight.

Chapter Six

Noah looks at me, and I can see the moment of disappointment flicker across his features. He thinks I've changed my mind, and I need to let him know I haven't. That I want this, him, perhaps more than I have ever wanted anything. I move towards him and grab his hands. I push him back towards the bed and make him sit. "Stop that thought," I tell him and kiss the end of his nose. "This is happening, Noah. I want you more than I can tell you."

I move back away from him and put my hands on the waistband of my jeans. I undo the zipper and let my gaze catch his as I start to shimmy out of the denim. He watches as more and more of my legs are exposed until I'm standing in front of him in just my lacy knickers. I creep back over to him and pull him to his feet. I trace my hands over the front of his torso as he stands there, staring at me, watching my every move intently, letting me do whatever I'm going to do.

My hands hit the waistband of his jeans. I undo his fly and sink to my knees in front of him as I slide them down his thighs.

"Fuck, Gem. You have no idea what a sight you are down on your knees," he breathes as I run my hands down his outer thighs, slowly undressing him.

I look up at him, lick my lips, and say, "Oh, I think I might," before placing a kiss on his hard cock through his boxers.

"Fuck!" His cock bobs in shock at the contact. I stare at the sight of him tenting his underwear, craving a taste of him, knowing how much I want to take him into my mouth. I help him out of his jeans and boots, and I look up at him. His breathing has quickened, and he stares at me with an intensity that I feel straight through to my clit.

I run my hand up his inner thigh. While returning the intensity of his look, I let my finger skim over the bottom of his balls and slip it between his legs to rub along the crack of his firm arse.

"Get in the middle of the bed," I command, my hand falling from between his legs to let him move.

Noah moves to the side of the bed and looks at me. I know what he's doing as he holds my gaze. He waits for my reaction as he slides his boxers down his legs, gets onto the bed, and grins at me. I know my mouth has just fallen open to an 'o', but it's difficult not to with the sight of such flagrant masculinity standing to attention directly in front of me.

I repeat his exclamation from earlier. "Fuck." I stare at his cock; it's bigger than I remember. For a split-second, I wonder if it's just that my memory of it has lessened, or if it actually has grown in the years I've not been familiar with it. I snap myself out of that pondering, and I gaze over all of him lying there on the bed, ready for the taking. I know exactly what I want to do with him.

"Spread your legs, Noah," I tell him as I put my knee on the foot of the bed and move towards him.

His legs part and allow me the space to get in between them. I feel like a hunter stalking her prey, keeping what I want firmly in my sights as I creep slowly up towards him.

I place my lips on the side of his right calf, and he moves a little, putting his hands behind his head like he's about to relax and just enjoy the show that I'm putting on for him. I give a little smile as I kiss up towards his knee and wonder how long his hands will stay where they are once I start doing what I plan to.

Once I reach his right knee, I move and kiss from his left calf up to his knee, and then move beyond. I softly kiss over his inner thigh until I hit just below his balls, and then swap back to the right leg, again climbing higher in a trail of kisses until I'm, again, just under his balls.

I stare directly at him and let my tongue caress the underside of his scrotum. He gasps, his cock jumping against his stomach, begging me for attention. I run my hands firmly over his thighs as I take one of his balls into my mouth and suck on it gently.

Noah groans, but his eyes never leave mine. I know he's drinking in the sight of me kneeling, sprawled out between his legs, my hands on his skin, and my tongue almost on the prize.

I can't resist anymore; I reach forward and lick the length of his cock from his balls all the way to the tip of his thick head. His breath stutters out of his body on a staccato exhalation. I'm flooded with memories of how good it sounds to hear this man moaning because of my mouth on his dick, and some of the other tricks that I had up my naïve little sleeves way back when.

I repeat the action and he hisses. "Fuck, Gemma. Stop teasing me and do it right," he begs, and I look at him with a grin and sink my lips over the head of his cock, lifting it with my hand to get a better angle to take him all in my mouth. I stare at him intently and slowly sink my mouth over his rock-hard length, eliciting a long moan from him.

"Fuck. Your mouth is better than I remember," he groans, his hand touching my face and running through my hair. When he hits the back of my throat for the first time, his hand knots in my hair, and he uses it to encourage my pace. I pull away from him and let him almost fall from my mouth before sinking over him once again. This time, his hips shift and he pushes deeper, the head of his cock pushing against my gag reflex. He stares at me intently.

"Christ, you look good with my dick in your mouth," Noah groans.

I run my hand over his balls and watch his eyes roll and close as he sucks in a breath. I bob my head up and down, sliding him in and out of my mouth, caressing him as I do.

I can't help but delight in the sweet sounds Noah is making under my influence. I run my tongue over the head of his cock and, at the same time, slip my index finger between his ass cheeks, hovering over his arsehole.

The next time the tip of his length hits the back of my throat, I push my digit against that ring of muscle, feeling it give way. As I rise and sink again on his dick, I start thrusting into him, matching the movements of my mouth, pushing him more and more, closer and closer with every move I make.

I look up at him and, again, his eyes lock on mine. My pussy soaks with the intensity of his gaze.

Noah watches me working him over. His breathing grows shallow and his fist tightens harder in my hair; he pulls slightly, not letting me take his full length to the back of my throat.

"You need to stop," he warns. The thought of him close to climax thrills me and makes me want to taste him all the more. "Gem, I need it to be inside you," he pleads. "God, after twenty years, I need to come inside you." His stare pierces through me and I lick the length of his cock before letting it slip from between my lips and slap back down on his taut stomach.

I remove my finger from his ass, and Noah grabs my hand and slips my index finger between his lips, sucking himself from my digits.

"Nice little trick." He smirks when he's done.

I grin. "You're not the only one to have learned a few things over the years."

He tucks his hands under my arms and pulls me up over his body so our faces are just inches apart.

"Oh, yeah?" he whispers against my lips as his mouth hovers over mine, threatening to claim it.

"Yeah." I grin again, and Noah's lips crush against mine, his arms pulling me tight against him. Every inch of him is pressed hard against every inch of me.

Without me realising what he's up to, Noah flips us so I'm beneath him. "My turn," he tells me, and sinks over my torso, placing his knee between my legs and pushing them apart.

When he finally gets to where he wants to be, Noah is resting with a shoulder against each of my inner thighs. I gaze down and see Noah's intense stare looking up at me. Without allowing me the chance to process what's about to happen, he slides his tongue the length of my soaked snatch.

"I've fucking dreamt about tasting you again," he murmurs against my sensitive flesh before sinking his long, firm tongue inside me. Holy fucking shit. Noah Redmond's mouth is firmly clamped over my pussy. Never mind Judgy Bitch having a stroke; I think I'm about to have one myself.

Uhhh is the only 'word' I have for him right now. He wasn't kidding; he really has learned some skills in the last almost twenty years.

Fucking Noah Redmond. Damn.

Chapter Seven

I've been wet and turned on since he jumped the queue in front of me at the bar. Kissing him and tasting him has only made the situation worse, and within what must be only thirty seconds of Noah's mouth sinking onto my pussy, I need to come, and I'm going to climax hard.

Whore. Judgy Bitch perks up. She's picked utterly the wrong moment to interfere. Her little utterance only makes it more of a turn-on, and I grab Noah's head between my thighs and hold him where he is.

His mouth is locked around my clit; my hips rise, seeking out more of his mouth. Just as I'm hovering on the brink of a monumental orgasm, Noah slides a finger inside me and curls it up against my G-spot.

I cry out, stars and colours spinning over the blackened backs of my eyelids. I grind against Noah's mouth, riding the waves of pleasure that just keep on going.

He lifts his head and, dazed, I look down to see his mouth and chin glistening with my juices.

"Oh, fuck, Noah," I breathe as I start to come down from my climax. He smirks at me, and I swear it's the sexiest sight I've seen. A shiver goes through me thinking of what his mouth just did.

Noah flexes his finger against my G-spot once more, and again, I shiver, a soft moan escaping my lips.

"Fuck, I love that sound. I've missed hearing it," he says fondly.

"I've missed you making me do it."

At my admission, Noah once again sinks his mouth over my sensitive cunt, licking and sucking me. He adds a second finger to the thrusting that he's begun with the first and alternates between circling and sucking my clit.

A second orgasm builds quickly and, again, I lock my thighs against him, holding him in place against me, needing to feel every single sensation he can tease from my body.

Noah takes me through my second climax, prolonging the feeling with skilled licks of his tongue and flicks of his fingers. When he's sure I've come down again, he removes his fingers from inside me. I hiss at their loss, and Noah puts his fingers in his mouth, savouring my flavour from them.

"Fuck, I've missed your taste, Gem. You're fucking delicious," he says before sliding all of his index finger into his mouth and sucking on it. The man is pure sex, and I need more.

Noah moves back over my stomach, kissing my skin. He stops at my breasts to give them extra attention, and I know it won't be long before he will have me coming again.

By the time Noah makes it back to my mouth, I can feel his length between my thighs. The tip of his shaft slides over my entrance, and we both hiss at the urgent need it starts within us.

"I need to be inside you, Gemma," he breathes across my neck as he nibbles on the skin below my earlobe.

I'm overwhelmed with lust for this man. "I need you there," I admit and feel his cock bob against me.

"I'll grab a condom," he tells me and goes to move away.

I'm overcome with a sense of loss the second I register his words. "Wait," I say, wrapping my arms around his neck and hooking my legs around his. The latter move has the benefit of pulling him against me, the head of his cock ready to sink into my wet pussy if he was to flex his hips.

"If I start this, I won't be able to stop, Gem," he warns me.

"I know," I tell him, holding his gaze, making sure he knows exactly what I mean. "I'm on the pill... Please," I almost beg.

"Jesus, Gemma." He sighs, his lips crushing against mine, his hips rolling upwards, his cock sheathing itself within my walls. We both moan at the feeling of his thick cock forcing my cunt to stretch out and accommodate him.

"Oh, Noah!" I breathe against his lips when he rolls his hips, withdrawing a little from me before sinking back in even deeper.

"I've been waiting for this," Noah says, and I'm not sure if he means for tonight or the past two decades. One thing is for sure; nothing has ever felt so right.

"I've needed it longer," I tell him, feeling a third climax starting to build, slow and intense.

"Not even possible," he argues, pulling back and thrusting in hard, his mouth finding my nipple.

I can't take it. It's like my nipple is directly wired to my pussy, and the second Noah's mouth connects with it, a chain reaction starts to tip me over the edge again.

My back arches, my hips flex against him, and my legs lock around the back of his, holding him tight inside me. Noah continues suckling on my tits and stars appear behind my eyes. I scream out his name as a powerful orgasm rocks through me.

Noah stops thrusting as my cunt clenches around his cock. "Oh, fuck yes, Gem. Come hard for me!" he encourages before taking my other nipple in his mouth. More shivers vibrate through me in response, and I'm suddenly overcome with emotion. Years of anger, frustration, and longing melt away with the fading of my orgasm, and tears well up in the corners of my eyes.

I open my mouth to explain to Noah, but he captures my mouth with his. His thumb finds my tears to sweep them away as he balances himself against me.

He starts rolling his hips and looks at me intently, his mouth no longer on mine.

"I know," he says, cradling my face. "I feel it too." More tears flood my eyes and my pussy clenches again, another orgasm looming. Just as I think I'm about to come again, Noah shifts against me, withdrawing completely, starving me of the friction I need. He moves to be on his knees and lifts my leg to rest on his body, my foot by his head.

Noah wraps his lips around my toes, and again, I feel it in my pussy more than I thought possible. He shuffles forward again, lining himself up against my cunt. His hands run over my leg, and he leans forward, the head of his cock pushing inside me. I watch him as he keeps his eyes fixed on what's happening between us.

He's watching himself slide into me, and I can't help but get even more turned on at the thought of what he can see. He thrusts hard into me, and the orgasm that had been impending returns. Watching him, watching us, watching us joining together.

I'm hyperaware of every sensation. This is no longer me fucking him, or him fucking me. No. This intensity only comes from making love to the person who is the other half of your soul.

Noah drives me through two more glorious orgasms before his own breathing changes and his intense stare is back. "I'm going to come, Gem," he tells me, and I know he's really asking me if it's still okay.

"Oh, God, Noah. Fill me," I purr at him. "Give me all your cum."

He grins slightly, drops my leg back beside him, and pushes himself in me, hard and deep; his whole body starts to shake. Hearing the delicious sounds coming from him, his more forceful thrusts bring me to the brink again with him, and we both reach that amazing crescendo together. I feel Noah flood inside me, knowing he has his cum deep inside me sending additional waves of pleasure through me.

Noah seizes my mouth with his and kisses me almost reverently, as the bliss continues to roll over us. He gradually gets heavier against me, his arms no longer willing to support him. "I'll get off you," he says, and I clutch him tight against me.

"Don't you dare move!" I growl. "Not yet. Lean on me; I don't care." Tentatively, he leans more of his weight on me. I lie there, stroking his back, feeling him against me, our bodies still joined together in the most obvious place.

This is what home feels like. All those people who said that their person felt like home, I never understood it until now. Intertwined with Noah Redmond at an age when I can genuinely appreciate it. Utterly divine.

Chapter Eight

When Noah finally tucked himself in beside me, we must have both dozed off in our sated state. I'm lying here, blissfully comfortable with his arm draped over my body and his warm, even breath on my neck as he sleeps beside me.

I glance over at him and I can't help but smile.

"What?" he asks sleepily.

I bite back a little chuckle. "Nothing."

"Then why are you staring at me with a smirk on your face?"

I shake my head. "How do you even know that? Your eyes are still closed."

"I know you, Gemma Elizabeth Reece."

You're not Reece anymore, Missy! Judgy Bitch starts. You'd better tell him, since you both seem to have forgotten you're married.

I wince at the thought, and he must feel the tension in me because he speaks before I have a chance. "Shut up. Gemma Elliott, I know, but you'll always be Gemma Reece to me." He opens his eyes and looks at me. "Sexy, beautiful, stubborn, bratty Gemma Reece." He smiles and kisses my neck.

"Oi!" I elbow him in the ribs, earning an *umph* from him in reply.

"And violent. Did I mention violent?" He smirks, holding his ribs where I 'injured' him.

"Asshole."

"Oh, yeah, and rude!" He grins.

I half fake a sulk and go to get out of the bed when Noah grabs me and pulls me tight against him, manoeuvring himself to be slightly above me. He presses his lips against mine before I can get any more complaining out, his tongue snaking over my lips, begging entry to my mouth. I can't resist and lick him back in reply; he penetrates my mouth with his tongue.

He releases my mouth from his and looks at me, his hand still cupping my face from our kiss. "Did I also forget to mention how fucking sexy you look when you're pissed at me?"

I glare at him, fighting a hint of a smile. "Yes, you might have missed that one too."

"Shame, because you really are so fucking hot when you're pretending to be mad at me."

I glare at him some more, and he tilts his hips against me, his hard cock pressing into me, and I realise he's not kidding. Apparently, I am sexy as hell when I'm pissed at him.

"Well, if I had known that, I would have showed you just how pissed I was at you when you fucked off to the army," I chide.

I'm a little surprised by the outburst. Noah looks like he was expecting it to come up, but perhaps not right at this moment.

"I was wondering when you would bring that up." He sighs and moves back to let me move if I want to.

"I don't want to go over it, I just want the chance to say how much it hurt me, how much I wanted you. I thought you were the one, Noah, and you left me."

He flops on the bed beside me on his back and runs his hand over his face. "I know I did, Gem." He glances in my direction. "And when you told me you were getting married, it shredded my heart. I knew I would regret my choice forever."

"I would have left him if you had asked me to." I can feel the evils from Judgy Bitch. I clamp my hand over my mouth, regretting saying it the second I do.

"And now?" he asks me with a vulnerable edge to his voice.

I roll towards him and look at him. "It's been twenty years and I'm a happily married woman."

He swallows hard, thinking about his next comment carefully. "Then why are you here?" There's something in his eyes that is almost begging me to admit it's because I still want to be with him.

"Because it's you, and you're... you're you," I reply, it's not the most definitive of replies, but it's the only answer I have to give him. I was, I mean *am*, a happily married woman. I love my husband; we've been together a long time. But Noah Redmond is something entirely different. He's just... him.

A hint of a smile graces his features. "Are you saying I'm irresistible?"

I shake my head and sigh, laughing. "You are incorrigible!"

"I am, but that's why you love me!" He grins.

I smile back, but I can't answer that, because he's right. I do love him. I think I always have, and that thought terrifies me. Instead, I distract myself with him, leaning over and kissing him. He responds by pulling me against him. I feel him growing hard again, and I can't wait to have him back where he was meant to be. Deep inside me.

Chapter Nine

A few hours' sleep and a whole lot of orgasms later, it's morning. I wake again with Noah's arm draped over my body and the rest of him is pressed against my back. I run my hand over his and press my ass back against him, loving how well we seem to fit together.

His hand moves over my stomach, running up my torso until he cups my breast. He nuzzles against my shoulder, nipping at my bare skin, his hard cock pressing against the crack of my arse. His fingers find my nipple, and I push my ass against him on a sigh. Noah nibbles harder on my shoulder, enticing a moan from me. His hand drops from my breast to my groin, and he runs a finger between my legs, over my clit. I grind back against his cock and he sighs against my neck.

I slip my hand behind him and grab his ass as he grinds his cock along the length of my arse. He breaks contact with my clit, reaching between us to position his cock against my asshole. He pushes himself against me, and his hand goes back to my clit.

Noah starts to rub himself against my arsehole, mixing

pressure against it with his cock and the circling of his fingers on my clit. He gets me so hot for him that I find myself pushing back against him; I want him. I want him in my arse. I need him to have taken me everywhere. I feel engulfed by a primal need to have him own every inch of me before I have to leave. *And go back to your husband; remember him?* Judgy Bitch in my head perks up again.

My eyes roll back in my head, and I'm not sure if it's in response to her or the delicious burn that's going on with Noah's hands on me. "Oh, God, Noah," I moan as I feel my first climax of the day building. He pulls back a fraction, just enough for his cock to move past my asshole and slide right to my pussy. He moves his fingers from my clit to the tip of his cock and pushes it inside me.

The rising orgasm slams into me as Noah fills me completely. There's a slight discomfort as he stretches me out to accommodate him, and, fuck, it feels so good. I clench around him, my cunt soaks, and all I want him to do is take me harder.

As the tightening in my pussy eases, Noah starts a rhythm, which has him thrusting hard and deep with short strokes, pulling out very little before crashing back into me. I can feel him pushing against my cervix with each thrust and, God, I want more and more of him.

Noah takes me to the edge of pleasure and over it again and again. The notion that I never come this often or as easily with Daniel flickers through my mind for a moment, only to fade again as another orgasm threatens me.

This time, I cry out his name when my climax strikes. I whisper it over and over like it's a fucking prayer. Judgy Bitch is glaring at me, I know she is, but I can't help myself. I want Noah, and I really want him deep inside me. I want to feel him flooding me, I need to, and I realise that I'm going to have to ask him.

"Noah!" I breathlessly exclaim.

He plunges hard against my cervix again and raises a long moan from me. "Fuck, Gemma!"

"Oh, God. Fill me."

"Don't you feel filled?" he asks, pushing hard against me. Fuck, I feel filled, but that's not the filled I mean, and I need to get enough clarity through the well-fucked fog that has captured my brain to get the words out.

"Fuck, Noah... I need your cum," I blurt out as the crest of another climax approaches.

A low guttural moan is the only reply I get. Noah's hand grabs my hip, and he slams hard into me. I feel that first spurt of his cum as he starts to unload deep in my cunt, and it's all I need to take me over the edge all over again.

We both come hard and lie there on our sides, panting as the ability to think rational thoughts, speak, or even move slowly returns to us. Not for the first time, Noah's cock remains buried inside me afterwards, and I relish that feeling. There is no haste; it's not a job to walk away from once complete. He needs that connection with me just as much as I need it from him.

I wriggle slightly, realising that, at some point, I will have to leave this bed. Noah's hand again pulls me tight against him. "Don't you dare move. Not yet." I melt in against him at his tone: sated yet possessive. He puts me at ease, and I want to prolong the bubble we exist in for as long as possible.

"I have to move," he murmurs against my back after a while. "I don't want to, but it'll be time to check out soon, and I need to have a shower and grab my stuff."

Reality washes over me, and when Noah pulls out of

me, I mourn the loss even more. A shiver runs through me and I suddenly feel the cool air of the room more harshly. I make a move to collect the covers and wrap them around myself, when Noah takes my hand. "Come shower with me," he says, and pulls me up, waiting for me to come with him.

I willingly leave the bed and accompany him to the bathroom. He kisses me softly and holds me tenderly against him. "This is the best way to start any day," he remarks as he adjusts the temperature of the water from the shower. "Get in," he tells me, holding the shower door open for me. I step in, and Noah gets into the shower behind me and closes the door.

I stand under the water, letting it wash over me, trying not to think about how this time with him is coming to an end. Noah moves behind me, pressing himself against me as he grabs a handful of body wash from the bottle in front of me.

"Put your hands up on the wall," he instructs me, and when I do, I am blessed with the feeling of his soapy hands rubbing all over my form. Again, feelings overwhelm me. Lifting my head to the water flowing down over me, I put my face in it as the tears start to fall, ensuring they're unseen.

Noah carefully and lovingly washes over every inch of me, cupping my sex and my breasts tenderly as he does. When he's complete, I rub my hands over my face and grab the bottle of body wash to repeat the intimate act on him.

Once bathed, we move in silence. We dry ourselves, stealing glances at one another. We dress, and I feel the end coming closer and closer. I step into the bathroom to clean my teeth and steel myself for what is about to happen.

When I leave the bathroom again, Noah is dressed and standing ready to go.

He moves towards me, his arms surround me, and he just holds me tight against him. Again, for one last time, the world around us fades away, and all that exists is us in this embrace.

Chapter Ten

Noah left after that. He said he would come back and we could share a taxi to the train station together, but I just couldn't do it. I couldn't prolong the agony of having him leave me again. Instead, I left before he got back.

I get on the train. I put my case in the overhead storage, park my ass on my seat, and stare blankly out the window. Now more than ever, I wish I had his number. I already regret leaving; I already know I want more.

My phone vibrates and I glance down at it.

> **Noah Redmond**
> If you thought you could just walk away,
> you forget that I know you, Gemma Reece.
> I put my number in your phone when you
> were in the bathroom and sent myself a
> message to get your number too, just in
> case.

Relief washes over me. I haven't lost him just yet. If you had asked me before last night, I would have told you I was a happily married woman, who would never even daydream about another man, never mind cheat on my husband. But last night changed that. Noah Redmond changed that. Truthfully, I have no fucking clue what is going to happen next. I love Daniel and I can't imagine there ever being a time when I don't have him in my life. But I have similar thoughts about Noah, or he wouldn't have spent the majority of last night buried inside me.

Some people say you can't possibly love two people at the same time; well, I think that's bullshit. Love comes in many different forms and flavours, and so do people. The only thing I'm sure about right now is that I love Daniel. I love Noah. And I don't think I can be without either of them.

I hit reply to the waiting message.

> Thank you xx

I hit send, returning my phone to my bag. Just as the train starts to move out of the station, I catch a glimpse of Noah standing on a different platform. He takes his phone from his pocket, looks at the screen, and grins before putting it back. I have no idea where this will lead, but, damn, it's going to be fun to find out. I never intended to cheat on my husband. I never intended to be a woman who was in love with two men. But here I am, starting an affair. In love with my husband, and already crazily in love with my lover.

* * *

Need to know how things end with Noah, Daniel and Gemma?

Read Desired, the completion of their story.

Gemma was happily and faithfully married until fate pushed her first love back into her life.

It should have stopped after one night, but the temptation for more was just too much. When her husband finds out about the affair she expected him to be hurt, betrayed, and that she would have to choose.

When it turns him on instead, suddenly she's given another option. Her lover and her husband. Suddenly she's never felt so desired.

About the Author

Dee Lish is an Irish author who loves to indulge her imagination with some filthy stories. She's been publishing under other pen names since 2014, but in 2023 returned to her erotic roots.

She likes to spend what little spare time she has binge watching her favourite shows, reading, and making messes and memories with her two children.

You can follow her on social media, or join her newsletter for all the latest naughtiness!

Also by Dee Lish

Succumb to Me Series

The Mistress

The Ponygirl

The Handled

The Punished

The Corrupted

The Student

One Handed Reads Series

Teased

Owned

Seduced

Tempted

Desired

Unexpected

Dee Lish also writes romance as Leighann Duncan

www.authorleighannduncan.co.uk

www.ingramcontent.com/pod-product-compliance
Lightning Source LLC
Chambersburg PA
CBHW030811190726
48285CB00003B/1130